Oi AaRDVARK!

Written by
Kes Gray

Illustrated by
Jim Field

*Hodder
Children's
Books*

"OI AARDVARK!"

said the frog.

"Come and be in my new book!"

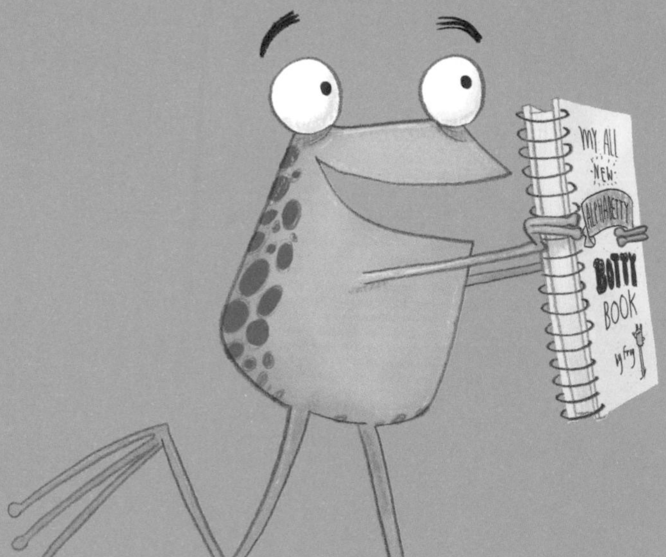

"It's called **MY ALL-NEW ALPHABETTY BOTTY BOOK,**" said the frog. "It's for animals I haven't told where to sit yet, I'm going to start with **A** for Aardvark and then go all the way up to **Z!**"

my ALL NEW ALPHABETTY BOTTY BOOK by Frog

"Good luck with that!" laughed the cat.

"What will **aardvarks** sit on?" asked the dog.

Aa

"**Aardvarks** will sit on **cardsharks!**" said the frog.

"What's a cardshark?" frowned the cat.

"It's a shark who's really good at playing snap!" said the frog.

"**B** next," said the dog. "What's an all-new animal beginning with B?"

Cc

And **crocs** can sit on **clocks!**"

"**D** next!" said the cat, "now you need to think of an **all-new D.**"

DOG!

said the dog.

"**D** definitely begins with dog!"

"D doesn't begin with dog. **Dog** begins with D," frowned the cat, "and anyway, we've done dog before!"

Dd

"We haven't
done **donkey!**"
said the frog.
"Donkeys
can sit on
long keys!"

"I wonder what
eels could sit on?"
said the cat.

F f

finches
can sit on
winches,

Gg

giraffes
can sit on **baths**

and **gazelles**
can sit on **bells!**"

"I wonder what **horses** could sit on?"
said the dog.

Ii

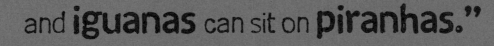

and **iguanas** can sit on **piranhas."**

"J and **K** next," said the cat.

J j

"**Jays** can sit on **maize**," said the frog.

"**Jays** can sit on **maize**,

jerboas can sit on **mowers**

Kk

and a **kudu**
can sit on some
doo-doo!"

"DOO-DOO!!!?"
gasped the dog.

"Doo-doo!"
grinned the frog.

"Any new Ls?"
sighed the cat.

Ll

"Llamas will sit on pyjamas

and lynx will sit on drinks!"

"Frog's really good at writing alphabetty botty books, isn't he?" said the dog.

"He hasn't got to **Z** yet," said the cat.

Mm

"**Mosquitos** will sit on **burritos,**

Nn

nits will sit on **banana splits,**

P p

"**Possums** will sit on **blossoms,**

pigeons will sit on **wigeons,**

pangolins will sit on **mandolins**

Qq

"Quetzels will sit on **pretzels,**

quolls will sit on **holes.**

Rr

Racoons will sit on **macaroons,**

Ss

Tt

turtles
can sit on
spurtles,

a **squid**
can sit on a **lid,**

Oo

otters
will sit on
swatters

and **orcas** will sit on
piggy porkers,"
said the frog.

"Frog's BRILLIANT at this!"
said the dog.

"Wait till you hear my new **P**s!"
boasted the frog.

Xx

"**X-ray tetra** will sit on seabeds, seaweed, seashells, coral, shipwrecks **et cetera!**" clapped the frog.

Uu

ticks
can sit on
wicks,

uakaris will sit on **saris.**

Vv

Vipers
will sit on **wipers**

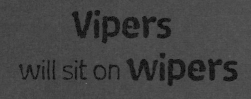

W w and **wombats**
will sit on **combats.**"

"Good luck with **X**," purred the cat.

and **pandas** will sit on **verandahs!"**

"You'll never think of a **Q,"** said the cat.

LIFT THE FLAPS!

Yy

"Yaks will sit on **sacks,**

and just to prove I CAN even think of a **Z** ... **zebras** will now sit on ...

Zz

candeLEBRAS!
A new type of black-and-white stripy candelabra that I've just invented!

NEW

Ta-dah!
My All-New Alphabetty Botty Book finished!" grinned the frog.

"Don't forget Zillyzinkzikkers," said the dog. **"Zillyzinkzikkers** sit on **frilly pink knickers."**

"Don't be ridiculous," said the frog, "there's no such things as zillyzinkzikkers."

"Yes, don't be absurd," said the cat.

"What are *they* then...?"
asked the dog.

The artwork for this book was made during the lockdown of the Covid 19 outbreak. I'd like to dedicate this book to the doctors, nurses, volunteers, shop-workers and delivery drivers who put their lives at risk to save and help others. Thank you! J.F.

To normality! K.G.

HODDER CHILDREN'S BOOKS
First published in Great Britain in 2020
by Hodder & Stoughton
This paperback edition first published
in 2021

Text copyright © Kes Gray, 2020
Illustrations copyright © Jim Field, 2020

The moral rights of the author and
illustrator have been asserted.
All rights reserved

A CIP catalogue record for this book is
available from the British Library.

PB ISBN: 978 1 444 95592 7

10 9 8 7 6 5 4 3

Printed and bound in China

MIX
Paper from
responsible sources
FSC
www.fsc.org   FSC® C104740

Hodder Children's Books
An imprint of Hachette Children's Group
Part of Hodder & Stoughton Limited
Carmelite House, 50 Victoria Embankment
London, EC4Y 0DZ

An Hachette UK Company
www.hachette.co.uk
www.hachettechildrens.co.uk

www.kesgray.com
www.jimfield.co.uk

Hachette Ireland
8 Castlecourt Centre, Castleknock, Dublin 15